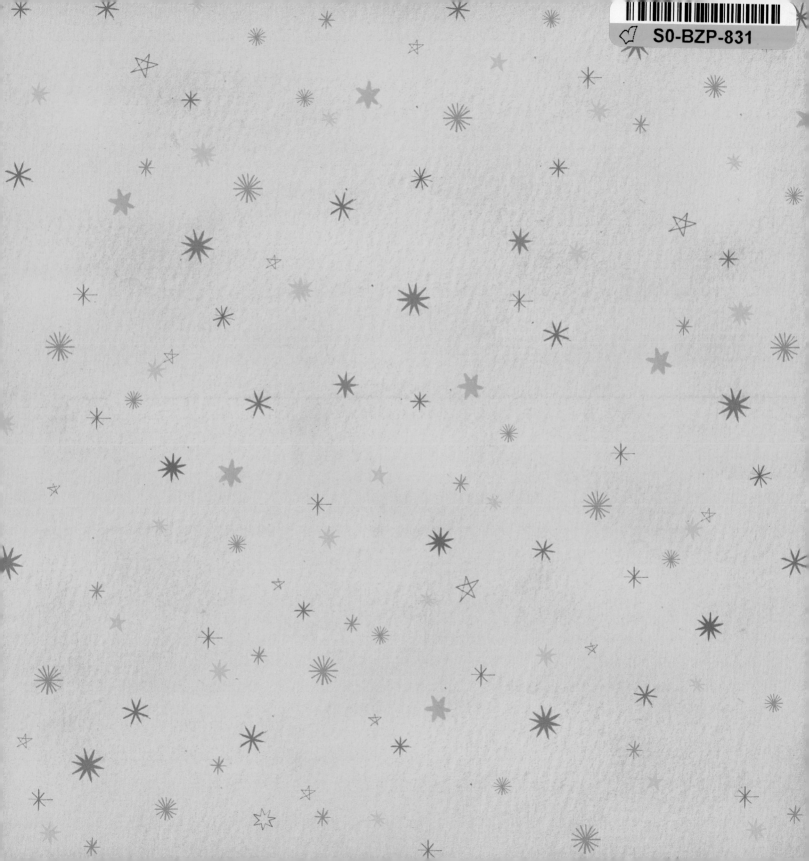

A World of Gratitude

Claire Saunders

Kelsey Garrity-Riley

*I would like to express my gratitude to Sunny Kulutuye, Gareth Williams,
Dwayne from Ngaran Ngaran Culture Awareness in Australia, the Kenya High Commission in London,
the Muurrbay Aboriginal Language & Culture Co-operative, and Tourism Fiji.
Many thanks to all of you for your kind help—Claire Saunders*

For Steven and Lisana, with much love and gratitude—Kelsey Garrity-Riley

First American Edition 2022
Kane Miller, A Division of EDC Publishing

A World of Gratitude © 2022 Quarto Publishing plc

For information contact:
Kane Miller, A Division of EDC Publishing
5402 S 122nd E Ave
Tulsa, OK 74146
www.kanemiller.com
www.myubam.com

Library of Congress Control Number: 2021949985

ISBN: 978-1-68464-457-5

Manufactured in Guangdong, China TT072022

1 2 3 4 5 6 7 8 9 10

MIX
Paper from
responsible sources
FSC® C016973

Contents

The Power of Thanks

What is gratitude? Is it just saying "thank you" when someone gives you a birthday gift? That's important, of course! But gratitude is a bit more than that: it's a feeling. Gratitude is noticing good things in your life, big and small, and appreciating them.

We can feel grateful for lots of different things: a gift, a bowl of juicy strawberries, a kind person who has helped us, a beautiful sunny day, a cozy bed we can snuggle into, and much more. And we can show our gratitude and appreciation in lots of different ways too, with words, gestures, and celebrations.

The amazing thing about gratitude is that the more of it we feel, the happier we are—gratitude is a superpower!

Did you know that September 21st is World Gratitude Day? All around the world, people celebrate the things they are thankful for.

THANK YOU

This book takes you on a journey around the world. You can find out how to say "thank you" in over fifty different languages, from Arabic to Xhosa. And you can also discover some of the wonderful ways people in different countries show gratitude to nature, animals, and each other. You may find out that not everyone shows their thanks exactly the same way you do!

This book also has tips on how you can practice gratitude yourself. Read about some of the different ways you can give and show thanks to other people, and discover how you can supercharge your gratitude superpower, simply by looking around you and noticing all the wonderful things in your life.

Some of the following pages teach you how to say "**thank you**" in different languages. For each language, this information is given:

The word for "thank you."

Merci
(MAIR-see)

How to pronounce the word.
The CAPITAL LETTERS tell you if there is a particular part of the word to emphasize.

EUROPE

The continent and the main country or part of the continent where the language is spoken.

FRENCH
Spoken in France

The name of the language.

Gratitude Signs and Symbols

You don't always need words to say thank you. Sometimes, you can use gestures or symbols instead. Here are a few examples from around the world.

The Hindu namaste greeting is used to show respect and gratitude in India, Nepal, and other parts of Asia. In the gesture, palms are pressed together in front of your heart, with fingers pointing upward. **"Namaste"** means "I bow to you."

To say thank you to someone using **American or British Sign Language**, move your flat hand from your chin toward the person you are thanking, and smile!

In Thailand, the **wâi gesture** is used to say lots of different things: hello, goodbye, sorry—and thank you! To wâi, put your palms together in front of your chest, then slightly bow your head so that your fingers touch your nose.

People in Japan bow to say thank you. The practice of bowing is called **"ojigi."**

Want to show your gratitude to someone in Hawai'i? **Shaka!** This friendly hand gesture isn't just used to say thanks, but also hello, goodbye, don't worry, hang loose, and generally "take it easy!" To shaka, make a loose fist, stick your thumb and pinky out, and gently shake your hand.

Whatever gesture or words you use to thank someone, it's nicest to do it with a big smile! Do you smile when you say thank you?

How to say...
Thank You in North America

This continent is home to 23 countries. It covers the frozen lands of northern Canada, the 50 states of the United States, Mexico, and the warm tropics of Central America and the Caribbean islands. The two main languages spoken are English and Spanish, but there are over 500 others spoken, too.

When **American** college students finish their studies, they often receive their diplomas at a special ceremony. Some students wear a piece of fabric called a Stole of Gratitude around their necks. Afterward, they give this to someone who has helped them during their studies to say thank you.

The **Native American Haudenosaunee peoples** begin and end important gatherings by saying the Thanksgiving Address. These beautiful words offer thanks to Mother Earth and everything in the natural world: other people, water, wind, thunder, plants, animals, the Sun, the Moon, stars, and more.

A wedding favor is a small gift that is given to guests at weddings to thank them for coming. In **Puerto Rico**, the married couple traditionally pins a ribbon called a "capia" to each guest to say thank you.

NORTH AMERICA

Mahalo
(ma-HA-lo)

HAWAIIAN
Spoken in Hawai'i

Nakurmiik
(na-koor-meek)

INUKTITUT
Spoken by the Inuit people
in Canada

Qujan (quoy-JEN)

KALAALLISUT
Spoken in Greenland

Thank you

ENGLISH
Spoken in the US
and Canada

Kinanâskomitin
(kina-NAS-komay-din)

CREE
Spoken by the Cree
First Nations people,
mainly in Canada

NAVAJO
Spoken by the Navajo people (also
called Diné) in the southwestern US

Ahéhee'
(uh-HYEH-heh)

Tlazocamati
(tlah-so-cah-MAH-tee)

NÁHUATL
Spoken by the Náhua
people in Mexico and
Central America

Mèsi
(MEH-see)

CREOLE
Spoken in Haiti

Gracias
(GRAH-see-ahs)

SPANISH
Spoken in
Central America,
Mexico, and the US

Maltyox
(mal-tee-OSH)

K'ICHE'
Spoken by the K'iche'
people in Guatemala

9

Gratitude Facts and Customs

Not everyone shows gratitude the same way. A custom that's polite in one country might seem strange in another. Here are some different ways people show thanks around the world.

Did you know that in some countries, it's polite to **NOT say thank you**? In China, India, and many other places, it's just assumed that people will do things for each other: if you help someone, one day they will return the favor and help you too! This means there's often no need to say thank you, especially to friends and family. In fact, thanking someone you're close to can be a bit rude, since it's seen as formal and unfriendly.

If you are given a gift, how do you show your gratitude? In some countries, such as Australia and the United States, most people say "thank you" or write a thank you note. But that's not usual in many parts of Asia and Africa. There, if a person is given a gift, they often show their appreciation by **giving a gift in return**.

Many cultures and religions around the world give thanks for their food before or after they eat. In Japan, it's common to start a meal with the word **"itadakimasu."** This expression gives thanks to all the living things involved in making the meal: from the plants and animals which provide the food, to the workers who harvested the crops, and the person who cooked. At the end of the meal, people say thank you once again with the words "Gochisousama deshita."

Tipping is a way of thanking people who have provided a helpful service, such as taxi drivers and waitstaff. In the US, tipping is very common. But other countries tip much less, and some don't tip at all.

Imagine you've just eaten a delicious meal. How do you show your appreciation? In China, letting out a **loud burp** at the end of a meal was traditionally seen as a compliment to the chef. In Japan, it's slurping that shows appreciation. Eating noodles with lots of noisy slurping sounds shows that you're really enjoying them.

Yum!

Next time you eat something— whether it's an egg, an apple, or a potato chip—think about all the people, animals, or plants that have been involved in its journey from the farm to your plate. That's a lot to be grateful for!

How to say...
Thank You in South America

South America is connected to North America at its northern tip, and stretches all the way south to the Antarctic. Many people on this continent speak Spanish or Portuguese, but there are also over 400 Indigenous languages—these are the native languages of people who have always lived here.

SOUTH AMERICA

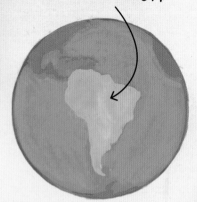

The Chachi people, who live in the rain forest in **Ecuador**, don't have a word for thank you in their language. Helping each other out is just something everyone is expected to do, all the time, so the word isn't needed.

Throughout South America, Mexico, and Central America, many girls celebrate their 15th birthday with a huge party called a quinceañera. In some countries, including **Argentina** and **Peru**, the birthday girl lights 15 candles, gives each one to an important person in her life, and thanks them.

Pachamama, or Mother Earth, is an important part of some people's lives in **Bolivia**. People show their gratitude to her with small offerings that can include leaves, flowers, and llama wool.

Tangi
(tan-gee)

SRANAN TONGO
Spoken in Suriname

Bedankt
(buh-DANKT)

Yuspagara
(yus-pa-gara)

DUTCH
Spoken in Suriname

AYMARA
Spoken by the Aymara
people in Bolivia and Peru

Merci
(MAIR-see)

FRENCH
Spoken in French Guiana

Sulpayki
(sool-PAY-ki)

QUECHUA
Spoken by the Quechua
people, mainly in Peru,
Ecuador, and Bolivia

Obrigado (if you are male)
Obrigada (if you are female)
(oh-bree-GAH-do /
oh-bree-GAH-da)

PORTUGUESE
Spoken in Brazil

Chaltu
(chal-too)

MAPUDUNGUN
Spoken by the Mapuche
people in Chile

Aguijé
(ah-we-JAY)

GUARANÍ
Spoken mainly in
Paraguay

Gracias
(GRAH-see-ahs)

SPANISH
Spoken in much of South America, including
Colombia, Argentina, Venezuela, Peru, Chile,
Ecuador, Bolivia, Paraguay, and Uruguay

13

Thanking Nature

All around the world, festivals celebrate and give thanks to nature. Many of these take place at harvesttime and have been celebrated for hundreds of years. People are grateful for a good harvest because it means plenty to eat in the cold winter months.

Harvesttime is when crops are gathered. In some countries, this happens in the fall, when many crops are ripe and ready for eating.

The **Homowo** harvest festival is celebrated by the Ga people of Ghana. People travel home to visit their families and enjoy a thanksgiving feast with dancing and singing. For a month or so before the harvest, no drumming or music is allowed in case it disturbs the crops—shhh!

The **Makara Sankranthi** harvest festival in India gives thanks to the Hindu God of the Sun, Surya, for helping crops to grow. People celebrate in different ways around the country, with fairs, bonfires, and kite flying. In a ceremony called **Bhogi Pallu**, harvest foods and flowers are scattered over children's heads.

The **Mid-Autumn Festival** (also called the Moon Festival) in China takes place in the fall, under the light of the brightest Full Moon. In the past, people worshipped the Moon and gave thanks for the harvest. Today, families gather to light lanterns, eat moon cakes, and appreciate the Moon's beauty.

Many Native American tribes in the US have harvest celebrations that go back hundreds of years. When the first corn ripens in summer, the Cherokee and other tribes celebrate the **Green Corn Ceremony**, with dancing, praying, feasting, and fasting.

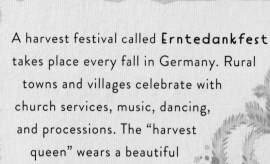

In the US, **Thanksgiving** is celebrated every year on the fourth Thursday in November. The first Thanksgiving was in 1621, when the Wampanoag Native Americans joined early English settlers in a three-day feast celebrating the harvest. Today, lots of Americans spend the day with their families, eating a dinner of roast turkey. Some people volunteer to help others too, for example, by organizing Thanksgiving food drives.

A harvest festival called **Erntedankfest** takes place every fall in Germany. Rural towns and villages celebrate with church services, music, dancing, and processions. The "harvest queen" wears a beautiful crown made from grains, fruits, and flowers.

In southern India and Sri Lanka's **Pongal festival**, cows have a special day just for them! Farmers hang garlands around the cows' necks and paint their horns in bright colors to thank them for their work in the fields.

How to say...
Thank You in Europe

Europe stretches from the Arctic in the north to the sunny Greek islands in the south. It's the second-smallest continent, but lots of people live here. Over 250 different languages are spoken across this continent.

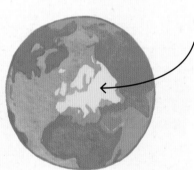

EUROPE

Go raibh maith agat (guh ruh MAH ah-gut)

IRISH
Spoken in Ireland

Danke (DAHNK-uh)

GERMAN
Spoken in Germany

Merci (MAIR-see)

FRENCH
Spoken in France

Gràcies (GRA-see-ehs)

CATALAN
Spoken in eastern Spain and Andorra

Grazie (GRAHT-see-eh)

ITALIAN
Spoken in Italy

Tack
(tack)

SWEDISH
Spoken in Sweden

Spasibo
(spa-SEE-ba)

RUSSIAN
Spoken in Russia

Dziękuję
(jen-KOO-yeh)

POLISH
Spoken in Poland

Dyakuyu
(DYA-coy-yoo)

UKRAINIAN
Spoken in Ukraine

Efcharistó
(eff-car-ee-STOH)

GREEK
Spoken in Greece

The **Italian** tradition of the "caffè sospeso" is all about showing gratitude for your own good fortune by doing something kind for someone else. The custom involves people paying for an extra cup of coffee when they're in a café. The extra coffee is then enjoyed by a stranger, or someone less fortunate.

In **Great Britain**, people say thank you 32 times a day on average—more than anywhere else in the world. How many times a day do YOU say thank you?

Maybe you can beat the record!

In **Russia**, people give flowers or other gifts to show thanks, and it's traditional to have an odd number of flowers in the bunch.

Thanking People

In our daily lives, lots of people help to look after us—our families, our friends, teachers, doctors, service industry workers, and other people in our communities. How do people around the world say thank you to these special people?

We often take our families for granted, but special days and festivals give us a chance to thank the people we love most! Many countries have a Mother's Day and a Father's Day, and some also have a Grandparent's Day and a Sibling's Day. In Ethiopia, the Gurage people hold a three-day festival for mothers, called **Antrosht**. Everybody dances and sings together, and eats a delicious feast.

The last Monday in May is **Memorial Day** in the United States. The day honors and shows gratitude to all the men and women who have died serving their country in the US armed forces. Many people fly the American flag as a sign of remembrance.

Many countries around the world have a special day to say thank you to teachers. But the Philippines has a whole month! During **National Teachers' Month**, children give their teachers beautiful flowers, read poems, and perform songs and dances.

During the **COVID-19 pandemic** in 2020, people from all around the world clapped, cheered, sang, or banged pots from their front doors or balconies. These noisy displays were a way to say thank you to all the brave people working in hospitals, grocery stores, transportation, and other important jobs.

Japan's **Labor Thanksgiving Day**, or **Kinro Kansha no Hi**, is celebrated each year on November 23rd. Young schoolchildren give gifts and homemade cards to police officers, hospital workers, firefighters, and other people in the community to say thank you for all their hard work.

Friendship Day is celebrated on different dates in different countries and is all about showing thanks to your friends. It's especially popular in parts of South America and Asia. In Argentina, young people get together with lots of friends to chat and have fun. Friends in India give each other colorful friendship bracelets to wear.

Which people are you thankful for in your life? Remember, you don't need to wait for a special day of the year to say *"thank you"* to them—you can say it at any time!

How to say...
Thank You in Asia

Asia is the largest of all the continents. About two-thirds of all the people on the planet live here—some in tiny villages, others in bustling megacities that are home to tens of millions of people. There are about 2,300 different languages spoken in Asia.

Mamnoon
(mam-NOON)

PERSIAN
Spoken in Iran

In **China**, tea drinkers tap their fingers on the table every time their cup is filled. This is to show gratitude to the person pouring their tea.

There are three kinds of thank you gifts you can give in **Japan**! Okaeshi are little gifts that you give in return for a present you've received. Ochugen and oseibo are gifts given in the summer and at the end of the year to say thank you to people who have helped you, such as neighbors or teachers.

Every day in **Bali**, people make little palm-leaf baskets filled with colorful flowers and place them on sidewalks and doorsteps. These daily offerings, called Canang Sari, express gratitude to the Hindu god Sang Hyang Widhi Wasa.

Toda
(toh-DAH)

HEBREW
Spoken in Israel

Shukran
(SHOO-kraan)

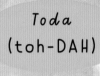

ARABIC
Spoken in much of the Middle East

ASIA

Gamsa hamnida
(GAM-sah ham-NEE-da)

KOREAN
Spoken in North and South Korea

Xiè xiè
(syeh-syeh)

MANDARIN
Spoken in China

Arigato
(ah-ree-GAH-toh)

JAPANESE
Spoken in Japan

Dhanyavaad
(DHUN-yuh-vaad)

HINDI
Spoken in India

THAI
Spoken in Thailand

TAGALOG
Spoken in the Philippines

Salamat
(sa-LAH-maht)

Khop khun krhup
(if you are male)
Khop khun ka
(if you are female)
(kob-khun krup /
kob-khun ka)

INDONESIAN
Spoken in Indonesia

Terima kasih
(te-RI-ma KA-see)

Famous Thank-Yous

Millions of "thank-yous" are spoken, written, and sent around the world every minute. Sometimes, one of them makes the news! Here are some famous and special "thank-yous" from history.

Every year, **Norway** gives a **Christmas tree** to Britain as a thank you for their help in World War II, when Norway was invaded by Germany. The tree is decorated with twinkling lights and displayed in Trafalgar Square in London.

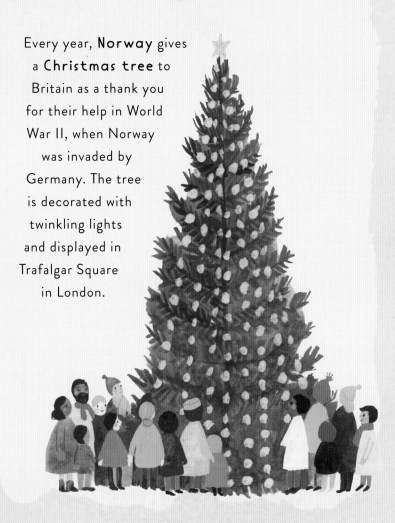

In 1969, **Neil Armstrong** became the first person to walk on the surface of the Moon. Twenty-five years later, he wrote a **thank you letter** to the team who designed his spacesuit, thanking them for the amazing piece of engineering that kept him safe in space.

Banksy is a famous British street artist whose graffiti has appeared on walls around the world. During the COVID-19 pandemic in 2020, an **artwork** by Banksy appeared in a hospital in the south of England showing a child playing with an action figure of a nurse. It came with a note from the artist thanking the staff for their hard work. Two years later, the artwork was auctioned for over £14 million! All of the money raised went to the hospital.

Imagine being thanked by the President of the United States! On National Teacher Appreciation Day in 2016, **President Barack Obama** thanked his fifth-grade **teacher**, Mabel Hefty, and teachers everywhere, for inspiring young people.

J. R. R. Tolkien was a famous English author who wrote the fantasy books *The Hobbit* and *The Lord of the Rings*. A few years before he died, Tolkien decided to thank his secretary, **Joy Hill**, for all her help over the years. But he didn't just give her a card or flowers—he gave her the ownership of one of his **poems**, called "Bilbo's Last Song." What a lovely way to say thank you!

After World War II, Europe was desperately short of food and other supplies. To show support, a journalist in the US organized a train called the **Friendship Train**. This set off around the US, collecting donations of food, clothing, and fuel, which were sent to France and Italy. In return, a French rail worker decided to organize his own train, called the "**Merci Train**" ("merci" is French for "thank you"). Tens of thousands of French people donated gifts—dolls, paintings, furniture, and more. These gifts of gratitude were sent in wooden boxcars to the US, one for each state.

How to say...
Thank You in Africa

Africa is the second-largest continent. Much of the northern part is covered by the world's largest desert, the Sahara. Africa is home to many different cultures and over 2,000 languages. Some people live in villages, others in big, busy cities.

In **Kenya**, a person visiting a friend's house will often bring a gift to say, "thank you for having me." This is generally something useful and practical, such as sugar, tea leaves, or soap. In return, the host will give their friend a gift to thank them for visiting.

Clapping, whistling, and jumping up and down—in **Zimbabwe**, it's common for people to show their gratitude using these gestures, rather than words. A clap of the hands is also used to say thank you in the neighboring country of **Zambia**.

The Yoruba people of **Nigeria** will sometimes kneel or lie down on the ground to show their gratitude to someone.

Shukran
(SHOO-kraan)

ARABIC
Spoken in much of
North Africa, including
Egypt, Algeria, and
Morocco

Na gode
(naa gaw-dey)

HAUSA
Spoken by the Hausa people,
mainly in Nigeria and Niger

Galatoomi
(gala-TOOM)

OROMO
Spoken mainly in Ethiopia
and Kenya

Daalụ or Ịmeela
(DAH-lu or ee-may-la)

IGBO
Spoken by the Igbo
people in Nigeria

Ameseginalehu
(a-muh-suh-ga-na-lahu)

AMHARIC
Spoken in Ethiopia

E se
(eh shey)

YORUBA
Spoken by the Yoruba
people, mainly
in Nigeria

Asante
(ah-SAN-tie)

SWAHILI
Spoken in East Africa, including
Tanzania and Kenya

AFRICA

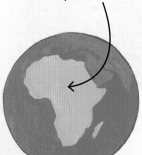

Enkosi
(en-KO-si)

XHOSA
Spoken by the Xhosa people, mainly in South Africa

Ways to Show Thanks

If someone gives you a gift, helps you, or is kind to you,
how do you show your thanks? You can say "thank you,"
of course, but here are some more ideas...

Thank you notes

Lots of people send thank you notes when they
are given a gift—you might have done this too.
Putting effort into writing a note or drawing a card shows
that you really **appreciate** the person and their kindness.
You can send thank you notes at **any time**, not just when
you are given something. Think about all the important
people in your life, and the kind and helpful things they do
for you. Next time a grandparent, a friend, or a favorite
teacher does something nice for you, why don't you write
or draw them a card to say thank you?

You can also write
thank you notes to
**people you don't
know**. Imagine what
your hometown would
be like without helpful
workers like librarians
and garbage collectors.
You could send a thank
you card to these
people too.

Acts of appreciation

We can show our appreciation for other
people with **actions**, as well as words.
For example, if a friend has been kind to
you, you could return the favor by lending
them one of your toys or playing their
favorite game with them. At home, you
might show your grown-ups how much you
appreciate them by doing a **chore**, offering
to help **cook**, or **cleaning up** after dinner
(without being asked!).

Thank you gifts

Have you ever given your teacher a present to say thank you at the end of the school year? Many people around the world give gifts to show appreciation. These don't have to be expensive: in fact, a **homemade** present can be the nicest gift of all because the person receiving it knows how much effort you have put into making it. Here are some ideas for homemade thank you gifts:

Paint a pebble

Decorate a glass jar
and fill it with flowers

Bake a cake

Pay it forward!

If something nice happens to you, one way to express your gratitude is to "pay it forward" by doing a **kind deed** for somebody else. Imagine how much kindness and gratitude there would be in the world if everyone did this.

How to say...
Thank You in Australasia

Australasia is the smallest continent. It includes Australia, New Zealand, and New Guinea, as well as some small islands in the Pacific Ocean. Fewer people live here than on any other continent, but they speak a lot of different languages—over 1,300 of them!

Aboriginal communities in **Australia** have a lot of respect for the land and nature. In southeast Australia, the Yuin Aboriginal people welcome Grandfather Sun as he rises in the sky in the morning. They thank him for his light and warmth, and for helping plants to grow.

In **New Zealand**, people have lots of ways to say thanks, including "ta," "chur," "sweet," and "tu meke" (a Māori phrase that literally means "too much"). Is there more than one way of saying thank you in your country?

In **Fiji**, one of the most important and valued objects is the tabua, a polished whale's tooth. This precious object might be given to thank someone who has done a lot for you, your family, or your village.

Palya
(PUL-ya)

PITJANTJATJARA
Spoken by the Aṉangu Aboriginal people in Australia

AUSTRALASIA

TOK PISIN
Spoken in Papua
New Guinea

Tenkyu
(tenk yoo)

Fa'afetai
(fah-ah-feh-tie)

SAMOAN
Spoken in Samoa

ENGLISH
Spoken in Australia
and New Zealand

Thank
you

Vinaka
(vee-NAH-kah)

FIJIAN
Spoken in Fiji

GUMBAYNGGIRR
Spoken by the Gumbaynggirr
Aboriginal people in Australia

Darrundang
(DAH-rroon-dung)
Meaning "you did well"

Malo 'Aupito
(mah-lo aw-PEE-tow)

TONGAN
Spoken in Tonga

Kia ora
(ki-OR-rah)

TE REO
Spoken by the Māori people
in New Zealand

Gratitude Tips and Exercises

Gratitude is a really amazing thing. When we make an effort to notice and appreciate the good things in our lives, it can actually make us feel happier. So, how can we start a habit of noticing all the good things?

Keep a gratitude journal

A gratitude journal is a special book for writing down (or drawing) the things you are grateful for every day. You could buy a notebook, or make your own by stapling together sheets of paper.

Every evening, think about your day and what you liked about it, then write down the date along with **three good things** that happened. For example, did you do or learn anything fun? Was anyone kind or helpful? What did you eat? Did you crunch in fall leaves, splash in puddles, or play in the sunshine? What was your favorite part of the day?

Make a gratitude jar

To make a gratitude jar, take a big, clean jar with a lid, and decorate it however you like. Keep the jar in a room that everyone in your home uses, with a pen and some slips of paper nearby. **Once a day**, each member of your family should try to write down something they feel grateful for and put the note in the jar. Every week, you can empty the jar as a family and read all the wonderful things that everyone has felt grateful for.

Go on a gratitude walk

When you are outside in nature, how often do you stop to notice and appreciate all the beautiful things around you? One fun way you can do this is on a scavenger hunt nature walk. Try to find or notice one thing in each of these categories:

✳ Something you can **see** (such as a colorful leaf, a furry caterpillar, a delicate spiderweb, or any of a million other magical things)

✳ Something you can **hear** (perhaps birds singing, a trickling stream, or the chirrup of a grasshopper)

✳ Something you can **feel** (like sand between your toes, warm sun on your face, or snowflakes melting on your tongue)

✳ Something you can **smell** (such as blossoms, pine needles, or salty sea spray)

More ideas

★ Create a big **collage** of all the things you feel grateful for, using photos, old magazines, and drawings.

★ Start **mealtimes** with an expression of thanks for what you are about to eat.

★ Play the **Alphabet Gratitude Game**. Take turns thinking of something you are grateful for, beginning with every letter of the alphabet.

★ Every day at mealtime, take turns with the other people in your family to **thank someone** sitting around the table.

Thank You!

This page is filled with reminders of some things to appreciate, but there are many, many more we couldn't fit on the page!

A beautiful sunset

Your favorite food

Your family pet

A soft, warm sweater

Giggling with your best friend

Helpful people in your community

Interesting books

A favorite cuddly toy

Crops, flowers, and trees

Animals big and small

Special days and celebrations

Snow days

Outdoor adventures

A hug from someone who loves you

Can you think of any other things that you are grateful for? Is there anything good about this moment, right now?